Contents

Some words are shown in bold, **like this**. You can find out what they mean by looking in the glossary.

What Are Clouds?

Clouds are made of billions of tiny drops of water called **droplets**. They can be white and fluffy or thick and gray. Clouds sometimes fill the sky.

4

Watching the Weather

Clouds

Elizabeth Miles

Heinemann Library
Chicago, Illinois

a division of Reed Elsevier Inc.
Chicago, Illinois

Customer Service 888-454-2279
Visit our website at www.heinemannlibrary.com

Designed by Richard Parker and Celia Jones
Illustrations by Jeff Edwards
Originated by Dot Gradations
Printed and bound in China by South China Printing Company

09 08 07 06
10 9 8 7 6 5 4 3 2

Library of Congress Cataloging-in-Publication Data

Miles, Elizabeth, 1960-
   Clouds / Elizabeth Miles.
         p. cm. -- (Watching the weather)
Includes bibliographical references and index.
ISBN 1-4034-5575-9 (HC), 1-4034-5673-9 (Pbk.)
1. Clouds--Juvenile literature. I. Title. II. Series.
QC921.35.M55 2005
551.57'6--dc22

2004002364

Acknowledgments
The author and publisher are grateful to the following for permission to reproduce copyright material: Alamy Images p. 27; Corbis pp. i, 17; Corbis/Charles & Josette Lenars p. 4; Corbis/Charles O'Rear p. 7; Corbis/Galen Rowell p. 11; Corbis/George Hall p. 25; Corbis/Jim Reed p. 13; Corbis/Lester Lefkowitz p. 26; Corbis/Pat Doyle p. 20; Corbis/RF p. 5, 18, 22; Corbis/Richard Hutchings p. 16b; Getty Images/PhotoDisc pp. 23, 16t; Getty/Taxi pp. 6, 9; Harcourt Education Ltd/Tudor photography p. 29; Philip Perry/Corbis/Frank Lane Picture Agency p. 24; Philip Parkhouse p. 28; Robert Harding Picture Library Ltd pp.15, 19, 21; Science Photo Library/Pekka Parviainen p. 10; SPL/Peter Menzel p. 12.

Cover photograph of clouds reproduced with permission of Corbis.

Every effort has been made to contact copyright holders of any material reproduced in this book. Any omissions will be rectified in subsequent printings if notice is given to the publisher..

Clouds form in skies all around Earth.
Winds blow the clouds around. Clouds
bring us all kinds of weather, such as
rain and snow.

clouds

This photograph
of Earth was taken from a
satellite. The white swirls
are clouds.

Different Kinds of Clouds

The names of clouds depend on their shape and how high they are in the sky. High, wispy clouds are called cirrus.

Cirrus clouds like these are sometimes called mares' tails because they are shaped like horses' tails. A mare is a female horse.

Different kinds of clouds go with different weather. You often see wispy cirrus clouds and low, puffy cumulus clouds in fine, sunny weather. Tall cumulonimbus clouds bring thunderstorms.

Flat, gray clouds like these are called stratus. They can bring rain.

Where Do Clouds Come From?

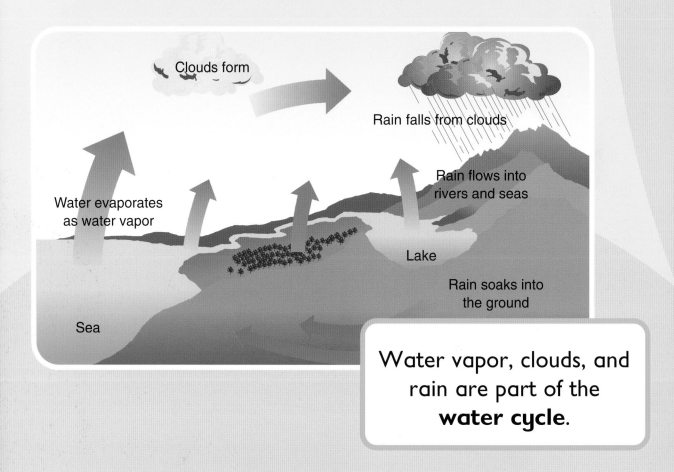

Clouds form

Rain falls from clouds

Rain flows into rivers and seas

Water evaporates as water vapor

Lake

Rain soaks into the ground

Sea

Water vapor, clouds, and rain are part of the **water cycle**.

Clouds come from **water vapor** in the air. As water vapor rises in the sky, it gets colder. Then it **condenses** into water **droplets**. These droplets form the clouds.

You often see clouds above mountains. This is because the air gets colder as it moves up the side of the mountain. Water vapor condenses and forms the clouds.

This mountain in South Africa is called Table Mountain. People say the clouds on top look like a tablecloth!

Studying the Clouds

When you see these fluffy, white cirrocumulus clouds it is called a mackerel sky. They look like the blotchy markings on a mackerel fish.

Meteorologists can study clouds to figure out what the weather will be like. Cirrocumulus clouds in the sky can mean wet weather is on its way.

Huge, towering clouds such as these, are called cumulonimbus. **Meteorologists** study these clouds because they sometimes bring thunder and lightning.

These clouds can sometimes bring stormy weather.

Measuring the Clouds

Meteorologists use many different ways to understand the weather. To do this they sometimes have to fly inside clouds to study them.

Special aircraft fly straight through storm clouds to collect measurements about the weather.

Weather balloons measure things like **temperature** and **humidity** in clouds. **Meteorologists** use the information to write weather forecasts for radio and television.

In this picture, weather scientists are launching a weather balloon into a thunderstorm.

Rain Clouds

Air is always swirling around in a cloud. The air gets colder as it rises and warmer as it falls.

Ice crystals form

Falling air warms up

Rising air cools

Water droplets

Rain clouds hold many tiny water **droplets**. At the top of the cloud it is very cold. The water droplets there may **freeze** into **ice crystals**.

Water droplets in a cloud join together and get bigger. When they are too big and heavy to stay in the cloud, they fall to the ground as rain.

Snow and Hail

Ice crystals such as these, stick together to make snowflakes.

Snow falls out of clouds when the air is very cold. Tiny **ice crystals** form at the top of the cloud. As they fall, the cold air stops them from melting into **droplets** of rain, and we get snow.

Sometimes, the water in clouds **freezes** and we get balls of hard ice called hail. When hail falls on the roof and windows it can make quite a loud noise.

A hailstone

Layers of ice

Most hailstones are at least the size of a pea.

Thunderstorm Clouds

Thunderstorm clouds are big, dark clouds that bring storms. Claps of thunder and flashes of lightning fill the sky. The flashes of lightning happen because of a buildup of **electricity** in the cloud.

The powerful heat from a flash of lightning causes a clap of thunder.

You should stay indoors during a thunderstorm.

During a thunderstorm, the sky becomes dark with thunderstorm clouds. Along with thunder and lightning, you often get strong winds and heavy rain.

Cloudy Views

This photograph was taken from an aircraft window. A thick covering of cloud hides the ground below.

You cannot see through a thick layer of clouds. When aircraft fly through thick clouds, the pilots sometimes use **radar** to find their way.

Fog is a low cloud that rests on the ground. It often forms during the night. In the morning, driving to work through fog can be dangerous.

It is hard for drivers to see other cars in fog. They must drive slowly to be safe.

Disaster: Tornadoes and Hurricanes

Tornadoes develop when the center of a giant storm cloud starts to spin. A twisting column of air stretches down from the cloud to the ground.

A tornado can destroy anything in its path.

During a hurricane, huge waves can sweep across shores and destroy boats and buildings.

Hurricanes bring storm clouds, heavy rain, and strong winds. They form over oceans and stretch for hundreds of miles. The strong winds can make huge waves at sea.

Unusual Clouds

Clouds can be very beautiful. Sometimes the water **droplets** in clouds break up the sunshine into lots of different colors.

These cirrocumulus clouds show shades of pink and blue in them.

People say that these kinds of clouds look like a pile of plates!

Clouds take on unusual shapes. They can look very lumpy or smooth, very flat or piled up. Mountain winds sometimes make piles of clouds called altocumulus lenticularis.

25

Is It a Cloud?

A low layer of dirty air over a city can look like a cloud, but is it? It might be smog. Smog is a mix of smoke and fog. The smoke comes from the city's factories, cars, and homes.

This shows smog over the city of Los Angeles, California.

An aircraft's narrow trail of ice crystals is called a vapor trail.

Planes high in the sky sometimes make trails that look like long, thin clouds. The plane's engines give out **water vapor**. This can **freeze** into a trail of **ice crystals**.

Project: Making Clouds

Ask a grown-up to help you. Never touch very hot water or it will burn you.

Clouds are made from **water vapor**. Try making your own water vapor at home.

You will need:
- a bathroom
- a sink
- hot water

1. Make sure your bathroom is cold.

2. Close the door and any windows, and block the sink using a plug.

3. Turn on the hot water faucet and let the sink fill with hot water.

4. When steam starts to fill the room, look at any cold surfaces, such as a mirror. Can you see any water **droplets** forming?

What happens?

Water vapor rises from the hot water. In the cold air, it **condenses** into water droplets to form steam. Bigger water droplets form on cold surfaces, such as mirrors. It is droplets like these that form clouds.

Glossary

condense change from a gas (water vapor) to a liquid (water droplets)

droplet very small drop of water

electricity form of energy. Many lights and machines need electricity to make them work.

freeze turn into a very cold solid. For example, water freezes into ice.

humidity measure of how much water there is in the air

ice crystal tiny bit of frozen water

meteorologist person who figures out what the weather is going to be like

radar equipment that uses radio beams to see objects ahead

satellite spacecraft that orbits Earth carrying equipment like cameras

temperature measure of how hot or cold things are

water cycle way all water keeps moving around as water on land, and in the air

water vapor water in the air. Water vapor is a gas.

More Books to Read

Ashwell, Miranda and Andy Owen. *Watching the Weather*. Chicago: Heinemann Library, 1999.

Chambers, Catherine. *Thunderstorm*. Chicago: Heinemann Library, 2003.

Jennings, Terry J. *Clouds*. North Mankato, MN: Chrysalis Education, 2004.

Sherman, Joseph. *A Book About Clouds*. Minneapolis, MN: Picture Window Books, 2004.

Index